Railway Series, No. 7

TOBY THE TRAM ENGINE

by
THE REV. W. AWDRY

with illustrations by
C. REGINALD DALBY

HEINEMANN · LONDON

HARTSFIELD J.M.I. SCHOOL

First published in Great Britain 1952
This edition first published 1995 for
The Book People, Guardian House,
Borough Road, Godalming, Surrey GU7 2AE
by William Heinemann Ltd
an imprint of Reed Children's Books
Michelin House, 81 Fulham Road, London SW3 6RB
and Auckland, Melbourne, Singapore and Toronto

ISBN 0 434 96675 4

Printed in Great Britain by
William Clowes Ltd, Beccles and London

DEAR FRIENDS,

Poor Thomas has been in trouble. So the Fat Controller asked Toby to come and help run the Branch Line. Thomas and Toby are very good friends.

Toby is a funny little engine with a queer shape. He works very hard and we are fond of him. We hope you will like him too.

THE AUTHOR

Toby and the Stout Gentleman

TOBY is a tram engine. He is short and sturdy. He has cow-catchers and side-plates, and doesn't look like a steam engine at all. He takes trucks from farms and factories to the main line, and the big engines take them to London and elsewhere. His tramline runs along roads and through fields and villages. Toby rings his bell cheerfully to everyone he meets.

He has a coach called Henrietta, who has seen better days. She complains because she has few passengers. Toby is attached to Henrietta and always takes her with him.

"She might be useful one day," he says.

"It's not fair at all!" grumbles Henrietta as the 'buses roar past full of passengers. She remembers that she used to be full, and nine trucks would rattle behind her.

Now there are only three or four, for the farms and factories send their goods mostly by lorry.

Toby is always careful on the road. The cars, 'buses and lorries often have accidents. Toby hasn't had an accident for years, but the 'buses are crowded, and Henrietta is empty.

"I can't understand it," says Toby the tram engine.

People come to see Toby, but they come by

'bus. They stare at him. "Isn't he quaint!" they say, and laugh.

They make him so cross.

One day a car stopped close by, and a little boy jumped out. "Come on Bridget," he called to his sister, and together they ran across to Toby. Two ladies and a stout gentleman followed. The gentleman looked important, but nice.

The children ran back. "Come on grandfather, do look at this engine," and seizing his hands they almost dragged him along.

"That's a tram engine, Stephen," said the stout gentleman.

"Is it electric?" asked Bridget.

"Whoosh!" hissed Toby crossly.

"Sh Sh!" said her brother, "you've offended him."

"But trams *are* electric, aren't they?"

"They are mostly," the stout gentleman answered, "but this is a steam tram."

"May we go in it grandfather? Please!"

The Guard had begun to blow his whistle.

"Stop," said the stout gentleman, and raised his hand. The Guard, surprised, opened his mouth, and the whistle fell out.

While he was picking it up, they all scrambled into Henrietta.

"Hip Hip Hurray!" chanted Henrietta, and she rattled happily behind.

Toby did not sing. "Electric indeed! Electric indeed," he snorted. He was very hurt.

The stout gentleman and his family got out at the junction, but waited for Toby to take them back to their car.

"What is your name?" asked the stout gentleman.

"Toby, Sir."

"Thank you, Toby, for a very nice ride."

"Thank *you*, Sir," said Toby politely. He felt better now. "This gentleman," he thought,

"is a gentleman who knows how to speak to engines."

The children came every day for a fortnight. Sometimes they rode with the Guard, sometimes in empty trucks, and on the last day of all the Driver invited them into his cab.

All were sorry when they had to go away.

Stephen and Bridget said "Thank you" to Toby, his Driver, his Fireman, and the Guard.

The stout gentleman gave them all a present.

"Peep pip pip peep," whistled Toby. "Come again soon."

"We will, we will," called the children, and they waved till Toby was out of sight.

The months passed. Toby had few trucks, and fewer passengers.

"Our last day, Toby," said his Driver sadly one morning. "The Manager says we must close tomorrow."

That day Henrietta had more passengers than she could manage. They rode in the trucks and crowded in the brake-van, and the Guard hadn't enough tickets to go round.

The passengers joked and sang, but Toby and his Driver wished they wouldn't.

"Goodbye, Toby," said the passengers afterwards, "we are sorry your line is closing down."

"So am I," said Toby sadly.

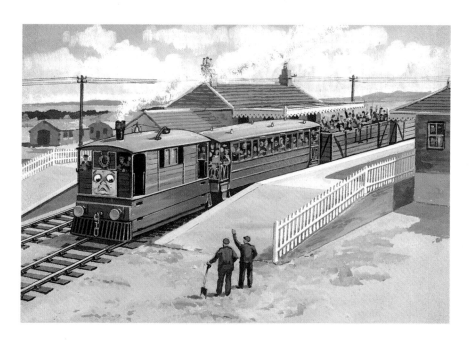

The last passenger left the station, and Toby puffed slowly to his shed.

"Nobody wants me," he thought, and went unhappily to sleep.

Next morning the shed was flung open, and he woke with a start to see his Fireman dancing a jig outside. His Driver, excited, waved a piece of paper.

"Wake up, Toby," they shouted, "and listen to this; it's a letter from the stout gentleman."

Toby listened and . . . .

But I mustn't tell you any more, or I should spoil the next story.

Thomas in Trouble

THERE is a line to a quarry at the end of Thomas's Branch; it goes for some distance along the road.

Thomas was always very careful here in case anyone was coming.

"Peep pip peep!" he whistled; then the people got out of the way, and he puffed slowly along, with his trucks rumbling behind him.

Early one morning there was no one on the road, but a large policeman was sitting on the grass close to the line. He was shaking a stone from his boot.

Thomas liked policemen. He had been a great friend of the Constable who used to live in the village; but he had just retired.

Thomas expected that the new Constable would be friendly too.

"Peep peep," he whistled, "good morning."

The policeman jumped and dropped his boot. He scrambled up, and hopped round on one leg till he was facing Thomas.

Thomas was sorry to see that he didn't look friendly at all. He was red in the face and very cross.

The policeman wobbled about, trying to keep his balance.

"Disgraceful!" he spluttered. "I didn't sleep a wink last night, it was so quiet, and now engines come whistling suddenly behind me! My first day in the country too!"

He picked up his boot and hopped over.to Thomas.

"I'm sorry, Sir," said Thomas, "I only said 'good morning'."

The policeman grunted, and, leaning against Thomas's buffer, he put his boot on.

He drew himself up and pointed to Thomas.

"Where's your cow-catcher?" he asked accusingly.

"But I don't catch cows, Sir!"

"Don't be funny!" snapped the policeman. He looked at Thomas's wheels. "No side plates either," and he wrote in his notebook.

"Engines going on Public Roads must have their wheels covered, and a cow-catcher in front. You haven't, so you are Dangerous to the Public."

"Rubbish!" said his Driver, "we've been along here hundreds of times and never had an accident."

"That makes it worse," the policeman answered. He wrote "regular law breaker" in his book.

Thomas puffed sadly away.

The Fat Controller was having breakfast. He was eating toast and marmalade. He had the newspaper open in front of him, and his wife had just given him some more coffee.

The butler knocked and came in.

"Excuse me, Sir, you are wanted on the telephone."

"Bother that telephone!" said the Fat Controller.

"I'm sorry, my dear," he said a few minutes later, "Thomas is in trouble with the police, and I must go at once."

He gulped down his coffee and hurried from the room.

At the junction, Thomas's Driver told the Fat Controller what had happened.

"Dangerous to the Public indeed; we'll see about that!" and he climbed grimly into Annie the coach.

The policeman was on the platform at the other end. The Fat Controller spoke to him at once, and a crowd collected to listen.

Other policemen came to see what was happening and the Fat Controller argued with them too; but it was no good.

"The Law is the Law," they said, "and we can't change it."

The Fat Controller felt exhausted.

He mopped his face.

"I'm sorry Driver," he said, "it's no use arguing with policemen. We will have to make those cow-catcher things for Thomas, I suppose."

"Everyone will laugh, Sir," said Thomas sadly, "they'll say I look like a Tram."

The Fat Controller stared, then he laughed.

"Well done, Thomas! Why didn't I think of it before? We want a Tram Engine! When I was on my holiday, I met a nice little engine called Toby. He hasn't enough work to do, and needs a change. I'll write to his Controller at once."

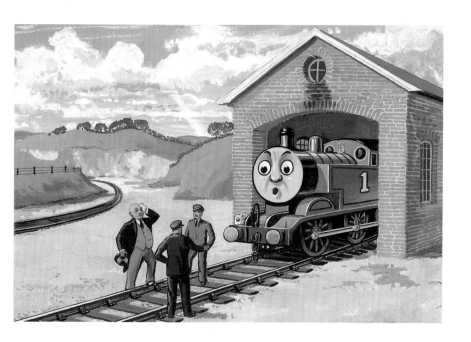

A few days later Toby arrived.

"That's a good engine," said the Fat Controller, "I see you've brought Henri tta."

"You don't mind, do you, Sir?" asked Toby anxiously. "The Station-master wanted to use her as a hen house, and that would never do."

"No, indeed," said the Fat Controller gravely, "we couldn't allow that."

Toby made the trucks behave even better than Thomas did.

At first Thomas was jealous, but he was so pleased when Toby rang his bell and made the policeman jump that they have been firm friends ever since.

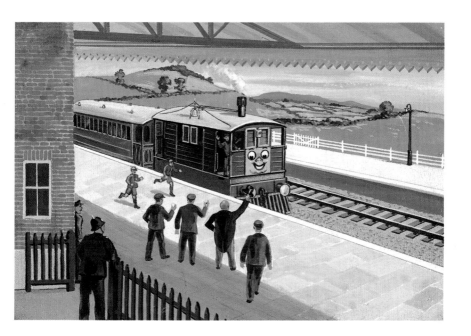

Dirty Objects

Toby and Henrietta take the workmen to the quarry every morning. At the junction they often meet James.

Toby and Henrietta were shabby when they first came, and needed new paint. James was very rude. "Ugh! What *dirty* objects!" he would say.

At last Toby lost patience.

"James," he asked, "why are you red?"

"I am a splendid engine," answered James loftily, "ready for anything. You never see *my* paint dirty."

"Oh!" said Toby innocently, "that's why

you once needed bootlaces; to be ready, I suppose."

James went redder than ever, and snorted off.

At the end of the line James left his coaches and got ready for his next train. It was a "slow goods", stopping at every station to pick up and set down trucks. James hated slow goods trains.

"Dirty trucks from dirty sidings! Ugh!" he grumbled.

Starting with only a few, he picked up more and more trucks at each station, till he had a long train. At first the trucks behaved well, but James bumped them so crossly that they determined to pay him out.

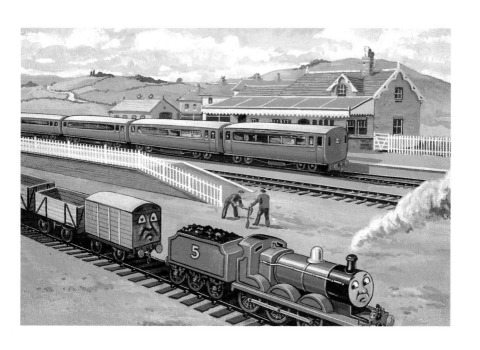

Presently, rumbling over the viaduct, they approached the top of Gordon's hill. Heavy goods trains halt here to "pin down" their brakes. James had had an accident with trucks before, and should have remembered this.

"Wait, James, wait," said his Driver, but James wouldn't wait. He was too busy thinking what he would say to Toby when they next met.

Too late he saw where he was, and tried to stop.

"Hurrah! Hurrah!" laughed the trucks, and banging their buffers they pushed him down the hill.

The Guard tightened his brakes until they screamed.

"On! on! on!" yelled the trucks.

"I've *got* to stop, I've *got* to stop," groaned James, and setting his brakes he managed to check the trucks' mad rush, but they were still going much too fast to stop in time.

Through the station they thundered, and lurched into the yard.

James shut his eyes ———

There was a bursting crash, and something sticky splashed all over him. He had run into two tar wagons, and was black from smokebox to cab.

James was more dirty than hurt, but the tar wagons and some of the trucks were all to pieces. The Breakdown-train was in the yard, and they soon tidied up the mess.

Toby and Percy were sent to help, and came as quickly as they could.

"Look here, Percy!" exclaimed Toby, "whatever is that dirty object?"

"That's James; didn't you know?"

"It's James's shape," said Toby thoughtfully, "but James is a splendid red engine, and you never see *his* paint dirty."

James shut his eyes, and pretended he hadn't heard.

They cleared away the unhurt trucks, and helped James home.

The Fat Controller met them.

"Well done, Percy and Toby," he said.

He turned to James. "Fancy letting your trucks run away. I *am* surprised. You're not fit to be seen; you must be cleaned at once."

"Toby shall have a coat of paint —— chocolate and blue I think."

"Please, Sir, can Henrietta have one too?"

"Certainly Toby," he smiled, "she shall have brown like Annie and Clarabel."

"Oh thank you, Sir! She will be pleased."

Toby ran home happily to tell her the news.

Mrs Kyndley's Christmas

IT was nearly Christmas. Annie and Clarabel were packed full of people and parcels.

Thomas was having very hard work.

"Come on! Come on!" he puffed.

"We're feeling *so* full!" grumbled the coaches.

Thomas looked at the hill ahead. "Can I do it? Can I do it?" he puffed anxiously.

Suddenly he saw a handkerchief waving from a cottage window. He felt better at once.

"Yes I can, yes I can," he puffed bravely. He pulled his hardest, and was soon through the tunnel and resting in the Station.

"That was Mrs Kyndley who waved to you, Thomas," his Driver told him. "She has to stay in bed all day."

"Poor lady," said Thomas, "I am sorry for her."

Engines have heavy loads at Christmas time, but Thomas and Toby didn't mind the hard work when they saw Mrs Kyndley waving.

But then it began to rain. It rained for days and days.

Thomas didn't like it, nor did his Driver.

"Off we go Thomas!" he would say. "Pull hard and get home quickly; Mrs Kyndley won't wave today."

But whether she waved or not, they always whistled when they passed the little lonely cottage. Its white walls stood out against the dark background of the hills.

"Hello!" exclaimed Thomas's Fireman one day. "Look at that!"

The Driver came across the cab. "Something's wrong there," he said.

Hanging flapping and bedraggled from a window of the cottage was something that looked like a large red flag.

"Mrs Kyndley needs help I expect," said the Driver, and put on the brakes. Thomas gently stopped.

The Guard came squelching through the rain up to Thomas's cab, and the Driver pointed to the flag.

"See if a Doctor's on the train and ask him to go to the cottage; then walk back to the station and tell them we've stopped."

The Fireman went to see if the line was clear in front.

Two passengers left the train and climbed to the cottage. Then the Fireman returned.

"We'll back down to the station," said the Driver, "so that Thomas can get a good start."

"We shan't get up the hill," the Fireman answered. "Come and see what's happened!"

They walked along the line round the bend.

"Jiminy Christmas!" exclaimed the Driver, "go back to the train; I'm going to the cottage."

He found the Doctor with Mrs Kyndley.

"Silly of me to faint," she said.

"You saw the red dressing-gown? You're all safe?" asked Mrs Kyndley.

"Yes," smiled the Driver, "I've come to thank you. There was a landslide in the cutting, Doctor, and Mrs Kyndley saw it from her window and stopped us. She's saved our lives!"

"God bless you, ma'am," said the Driver, and tiptoed from the room.

They cleared the line by Christmas Day, and the sun shone as a special train puffed up from the junction.

First came Toby, then Thomas with Annie and Clarabel, and last of all, but very pleased at being allowed to come, was Henrietta.

The Fat Controller was there, and lots of other people who wanted to say "Thank you" to Mrs Kyndley.

"Peepeep, Peepeep! Happy Christmas!" whistled the engines as they reached the place.

The people got out and climbed to the cottage. Thomas and Toby wished they could go too.

Mrs Kyndley's husband met them at the door.

The Fat Controller, Thomas's Driver, Fireman, and Guard went upstairs, while the others stood in the sunshine below the window.

The Driver gave her a new dressing-gown to replace the one spoilt by the rain. The Guard brought her some grapes, and the Fireman gave her some woolly slippers, and promised to bring some coal as a present from Thomas, next time they passed.

Mrs Kyndley was very pleased with her presents.

"You are very good to me," she said.

"The passengers and I," said the Fat Controller, "hope you will accept these tickets for the South Coast, Mrs Kyndley, and get really well in the sunshine. We cannot thank you enough for preventing that accident. I hope we have not tired you. Goodbye and a happy Christmas."

Then going quietly downstairs, they joined the group outside the window, and sang some carols before returning to the train.

Mrs Kyndley is now at Bournemouth, getting better every day, and Thomas and Toby are looking forward to the time when they can welcome her home.

Titles in this series